Fantasy I
TAHALA ISLAND

ART OF GUILLAUME TAVERNIER

There is no place on this island from which you cannot see the sea; directly or indirectly, all the smells of Tahala come from it. And be it the crashing of the waves or the screams of the birds, there is no way to escape its sounds either.

From an early age, the islander will run though the steep streets of Tahala, slaloming between fish carts, poustarra barrels and baskets of charme-nez. If he is a sailor's or a fisherman' son, it will not take long before he hops on a boat. And if he is not, he will still have learned how to fish, swim and dive like the other children of his age.

70 grande rue
La Barre en Ouche
27330 MESNIL EN OUCHE

SUMMARY

TAHALA

1 The palace
2 The door
3 The lighthouse
4 The bazaar
5 The temple
6 Villa Del Montir
7 The bakery
8 The herbalist
9 The dovecote
10 The dyeing house
11 The orphanage
12 The abandoned house
13 The mine
14 The elevator
15 The forge
16 The restaurant of the abysses
17 The hull repairer
18 The ice shop
19 The favourable winds
20 The prison
21 The slaughterhouse
22 The hemp grower
23 The bone engraver
24 The one-eyed cat inn
25 The hostel
26 The ink factory
27 The sail factory
28 The botanist
29 The dispensary
30 The stone quarry

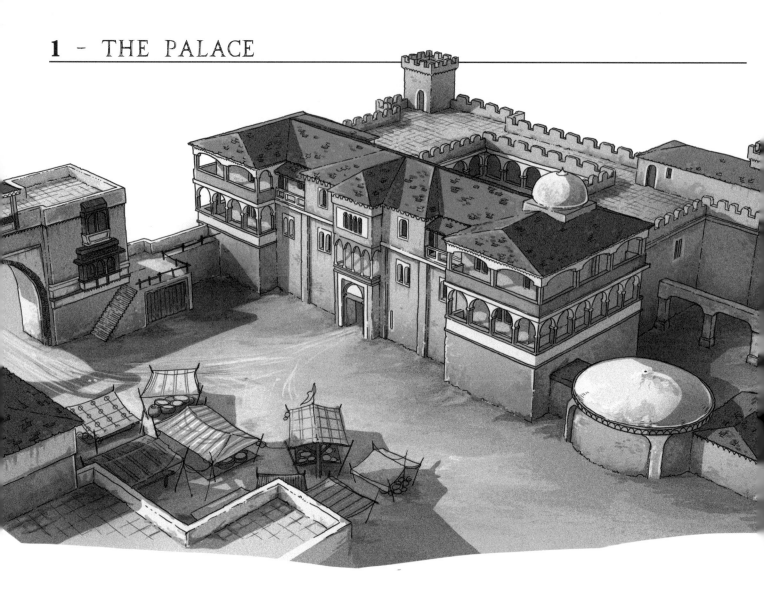

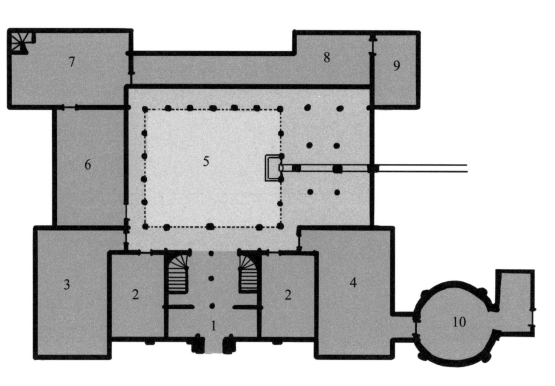

Ground floor

1 Hall
2 Scribes
3 Administrator of the city
4 Office
5 Waiting room
6 Treasurer's Office
7 Meeting room
8 Archives
9 Reserve
10 Palace Factotum

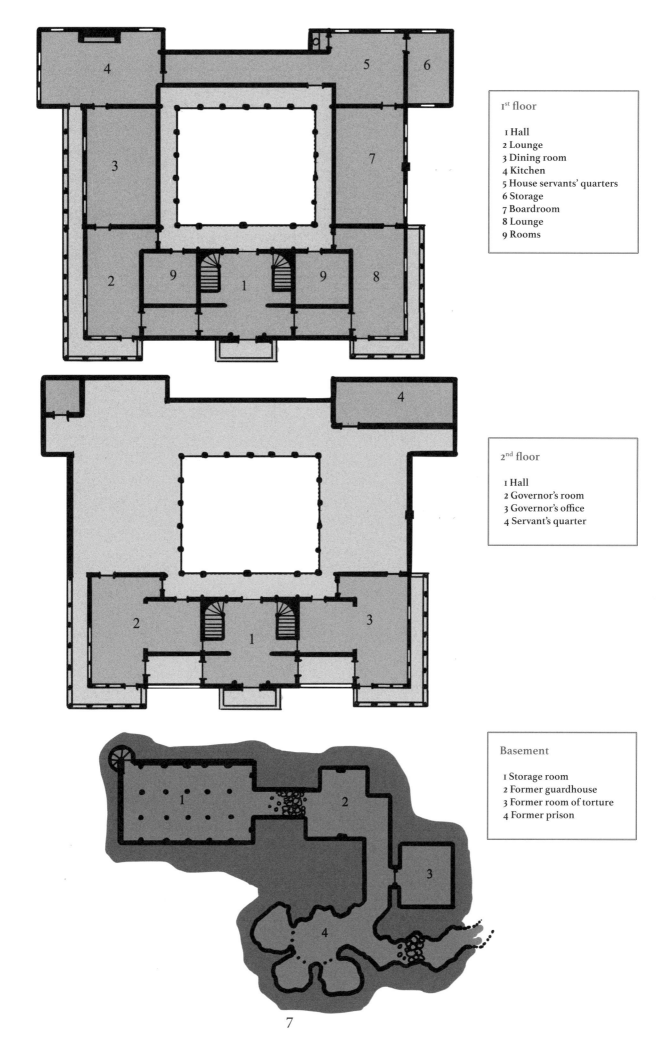

1st floor

1 Hall
2 Lounge
3 Dining room
4 Kitchen
5 House servants' quarters
6 Storage
7 Boardroom
8 Lounge
9 Rooms

2nd floor

1 Hall
2 Governor's room
3 Governor's office
4 Servant's quarter

Basement

1 Storage room
2 Former guardhouse
3 Former room of torture
4 Former prison

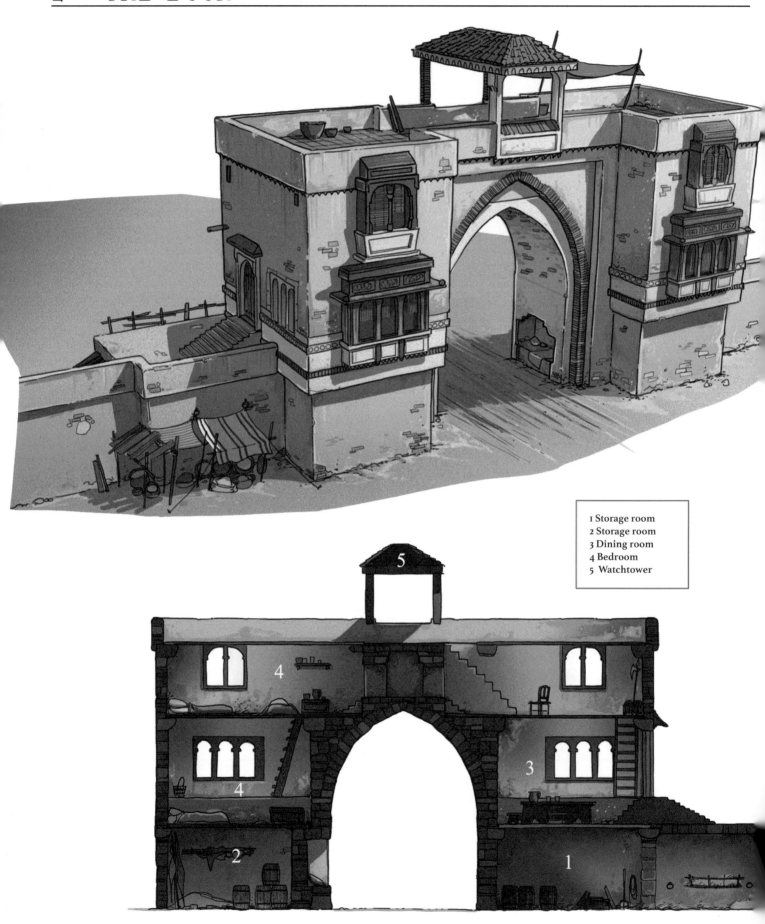

1 Storage room
2 Storage room
3 Dining room
4 Bedroom
5 Watchtower

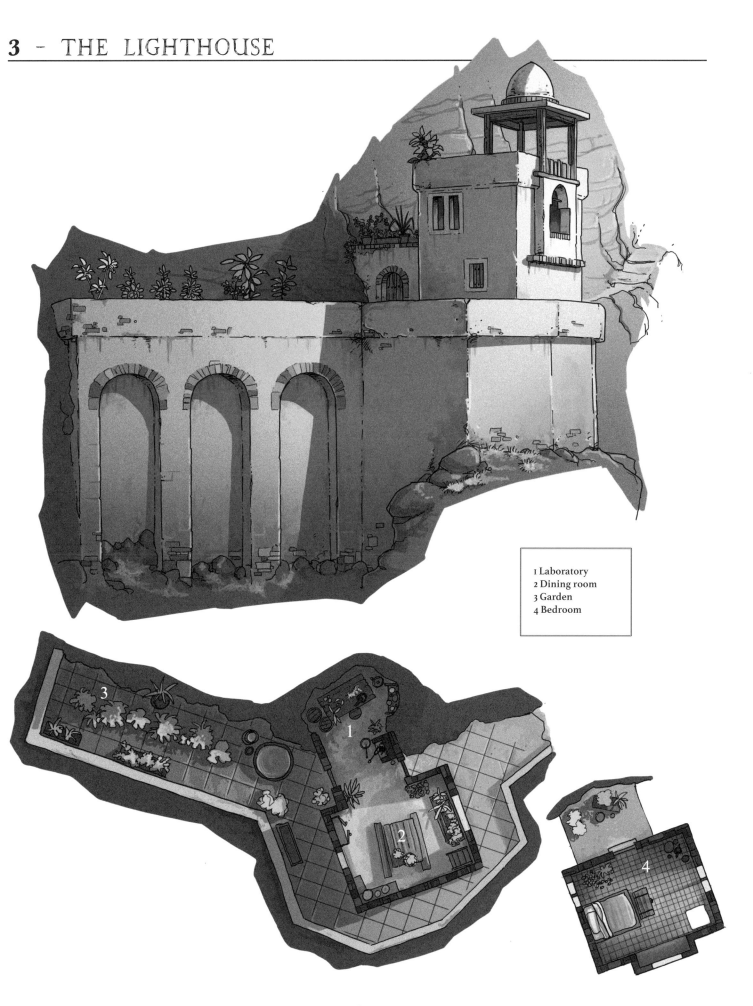

1 Laboratory
2 Dining room
3 Garden
4 Bedroom

1 Shop
2 Dining room
3 Bedroom
4 Bedroom

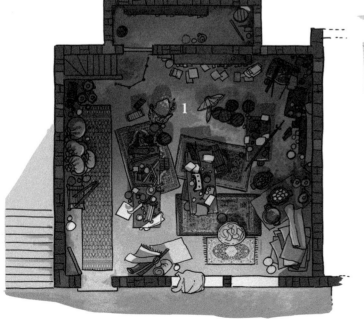

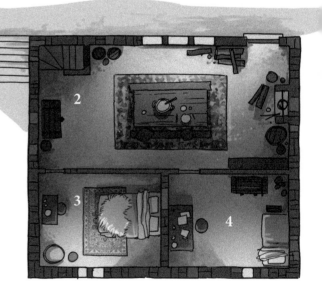

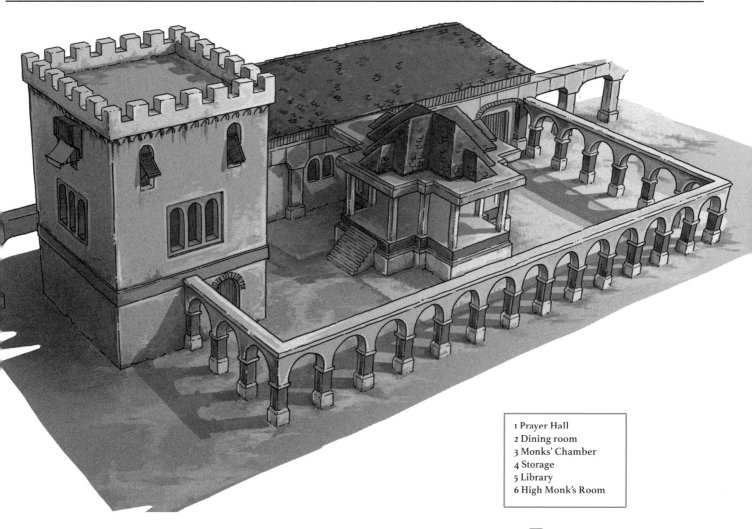

1 Prayer Hall
2 Dining room
3 Monks' Chamber
4 Storage
5 Library
6 High Monk's Room

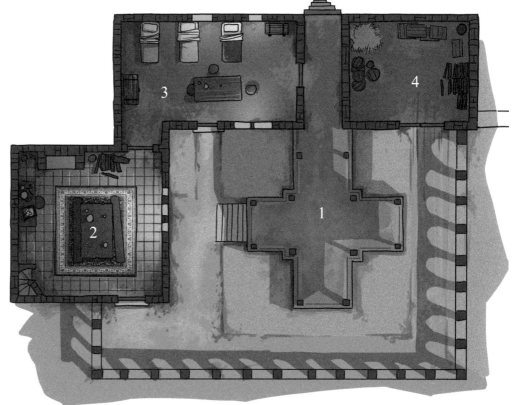

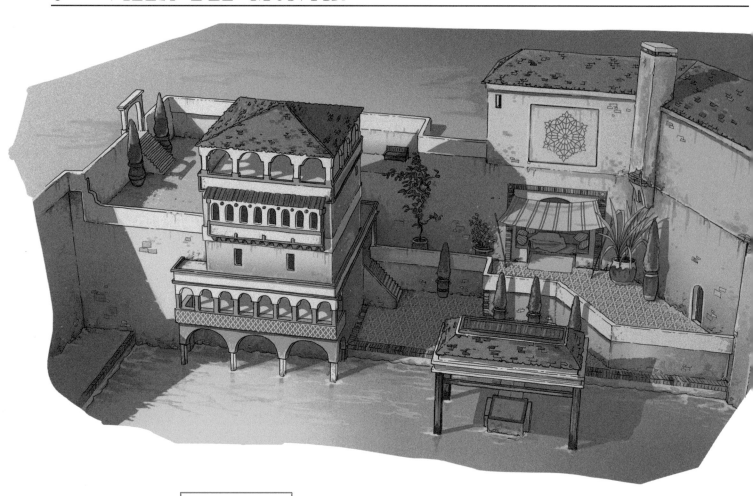

1 Dining room
2 Office
3 Storage
4 Storage
5 Servants' room
6 Servants' bedroom

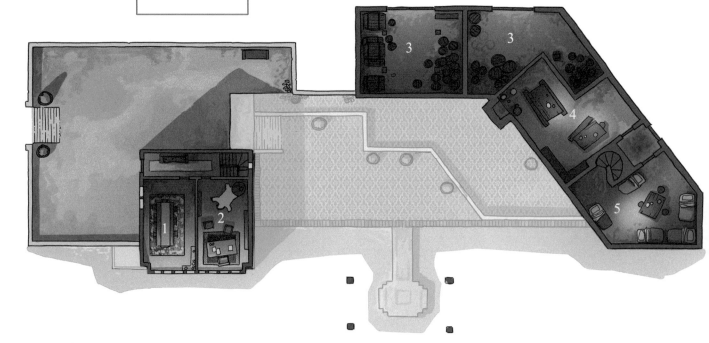

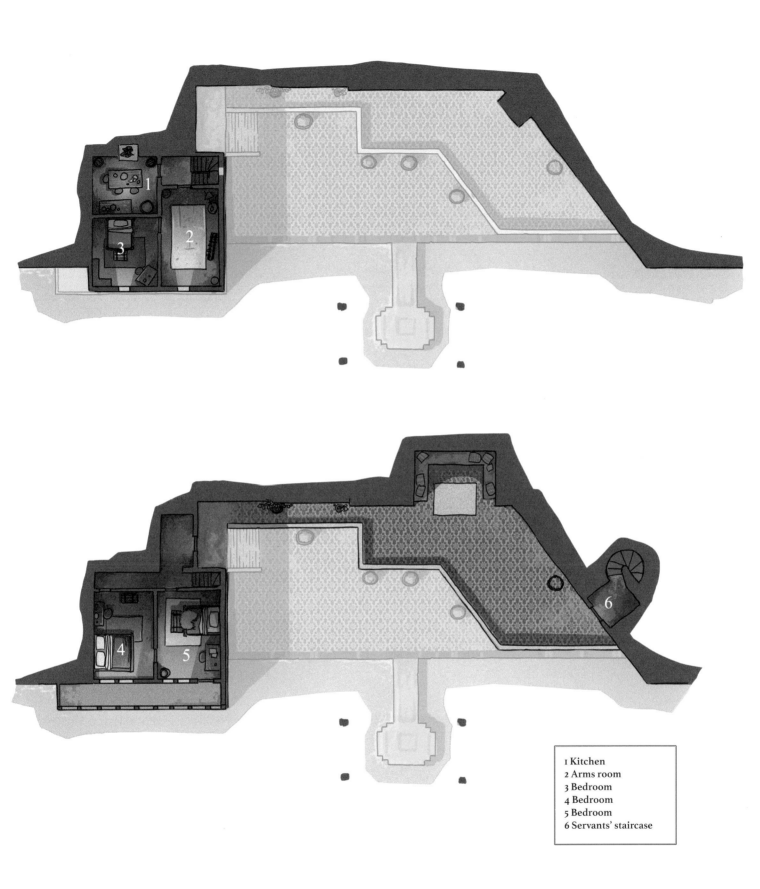

1 Kitchen
2 Arms room
3 Bedroom
4 Bedroom
5 Bedroom
6 Servants' staircase

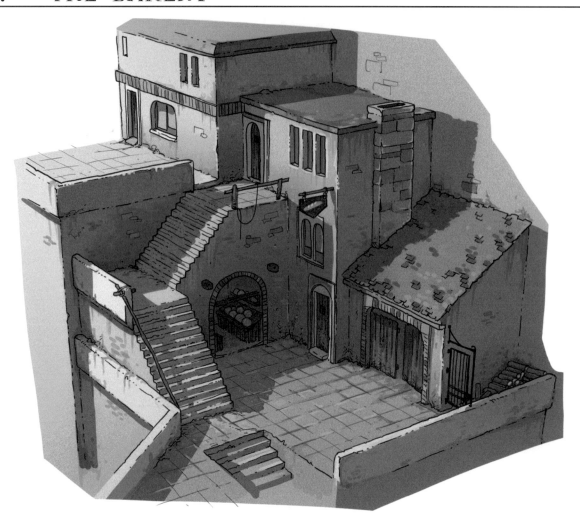

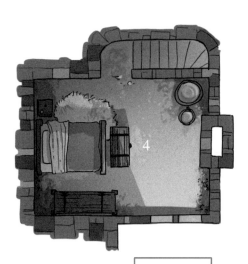

1 Bakery
2 Store
3 Room
4 Bedroom

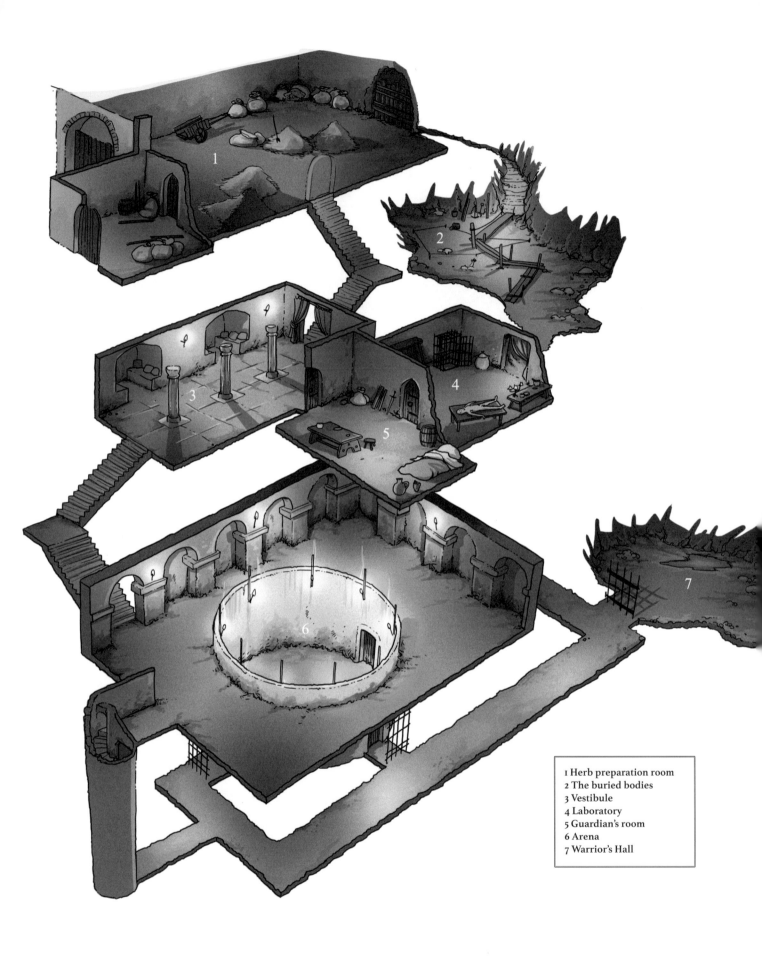

1 Herb preparation room
2 The buried bodies
3 Vestibule
4 Laboratory
5 Guardian's room
6 Arena
7 Warrior's Hall

1 Room
2 Bedroom
3 Storage
4 Flight room

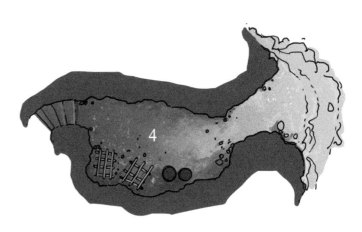

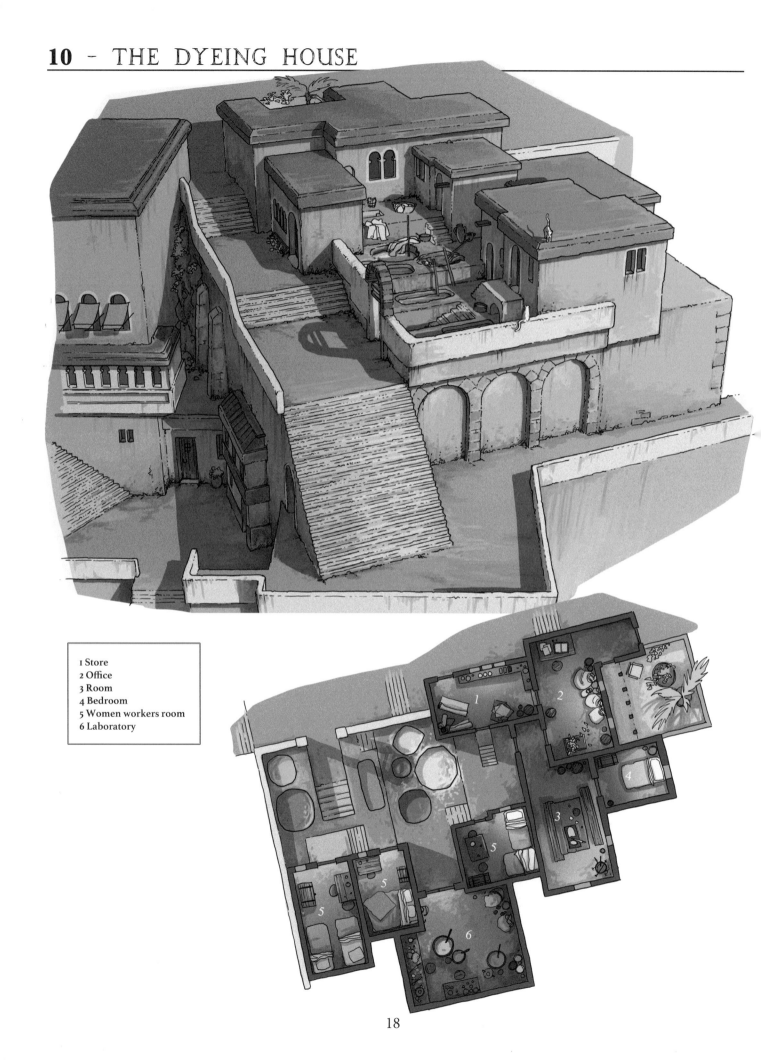

1 Store
2 Office
3 Room
4 Bedroom
5 Women workers room
6 Laboratory

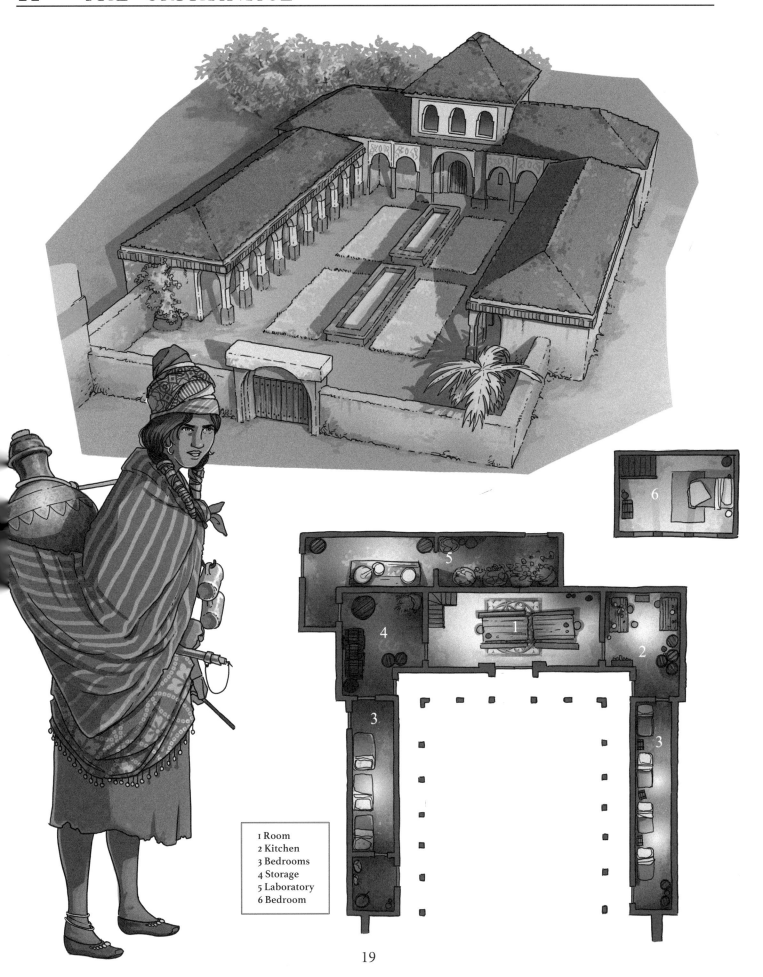

1 Room
2 Kitchen
3 Bedrooms
4 Storage
5 Laboratory
6 Bedroom

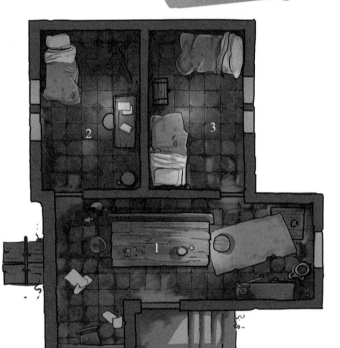

1 Room
2 Bedroom
3 Bedroom
4 Cellar
5 Secret room
6 Secret corridor

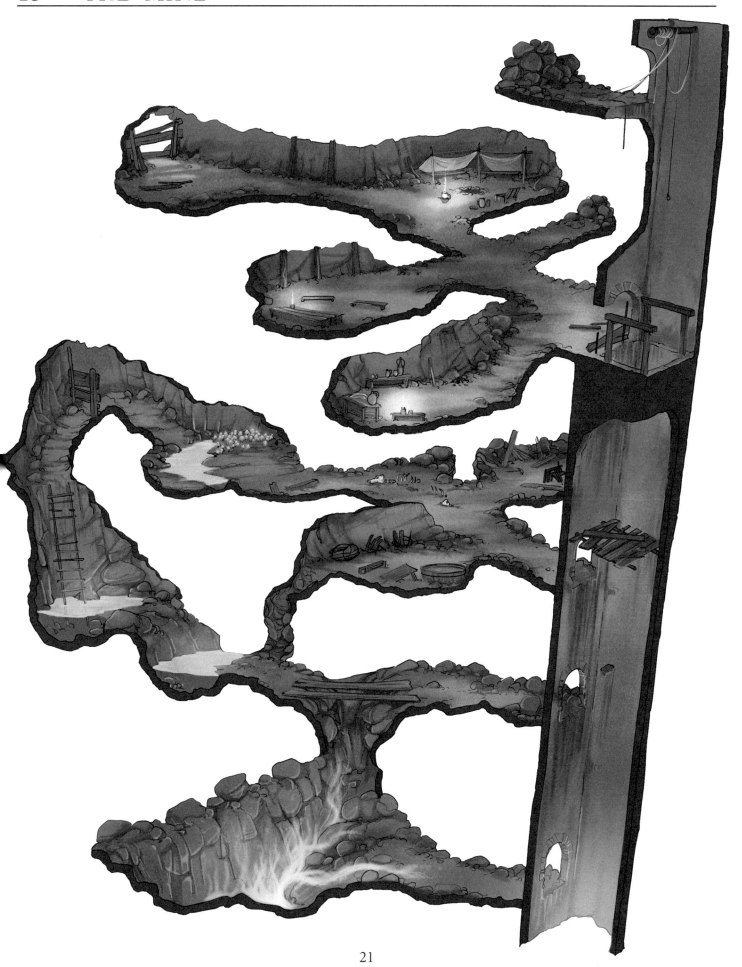

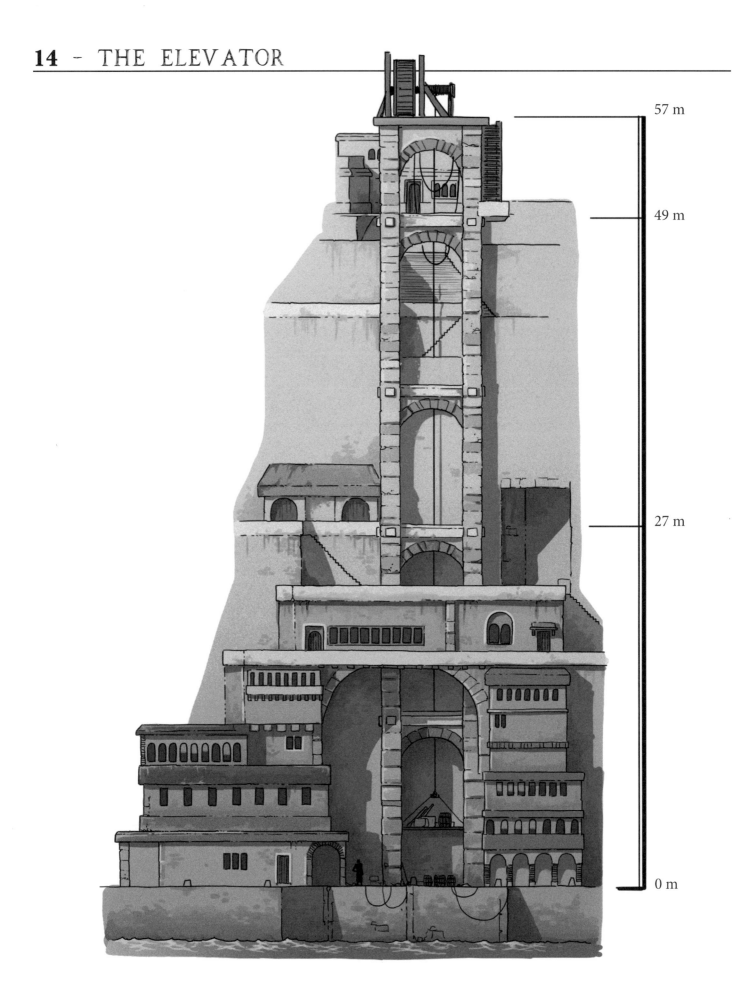

57 m

49 m

27 m

0 m

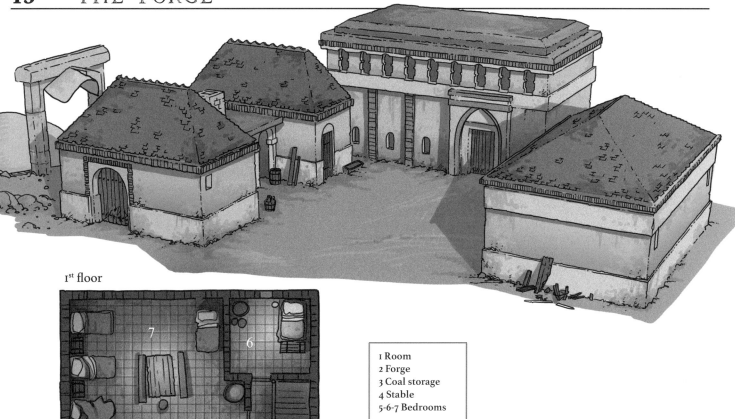

1ˢᵗ floor

1 Room
2 Forge
3 Coal storage
4 Stable
5-6-7 Bedrooms

Ground floor

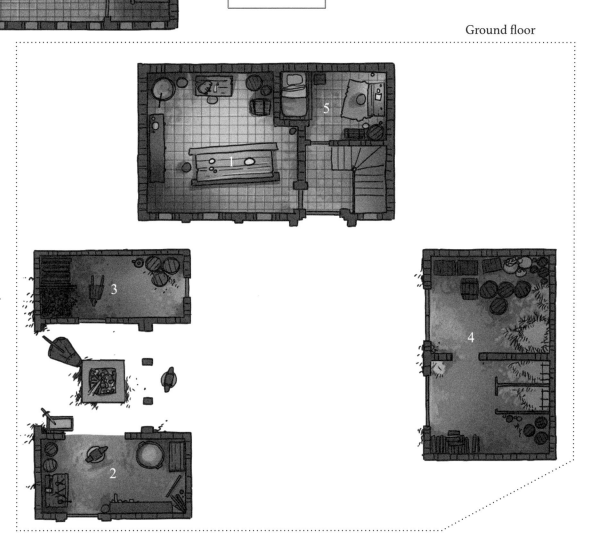

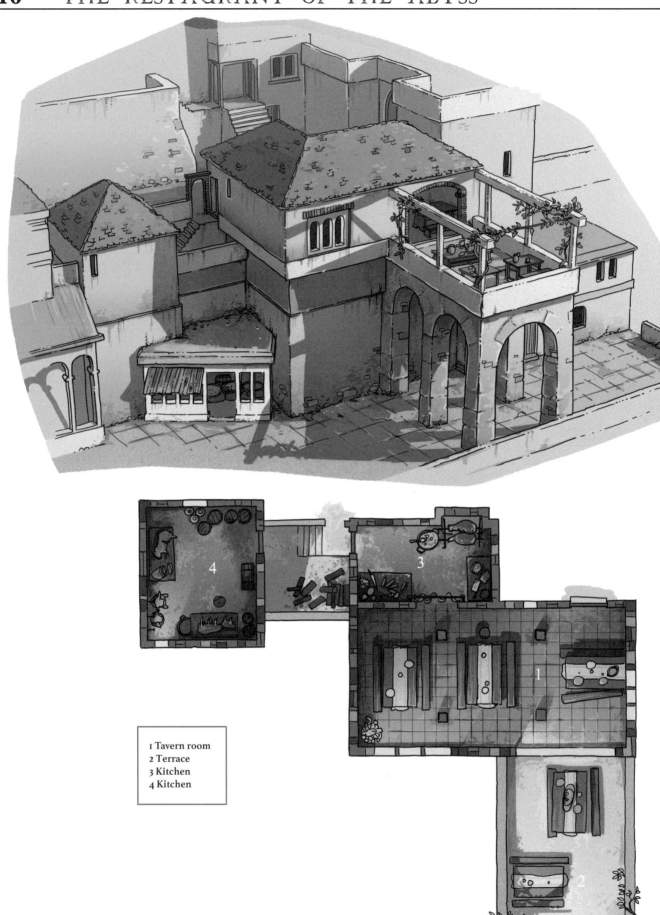

1 Tavern room
2 Terrace
3 Kitchen
4 Kitchen

17 - THE HULL REPAIRER

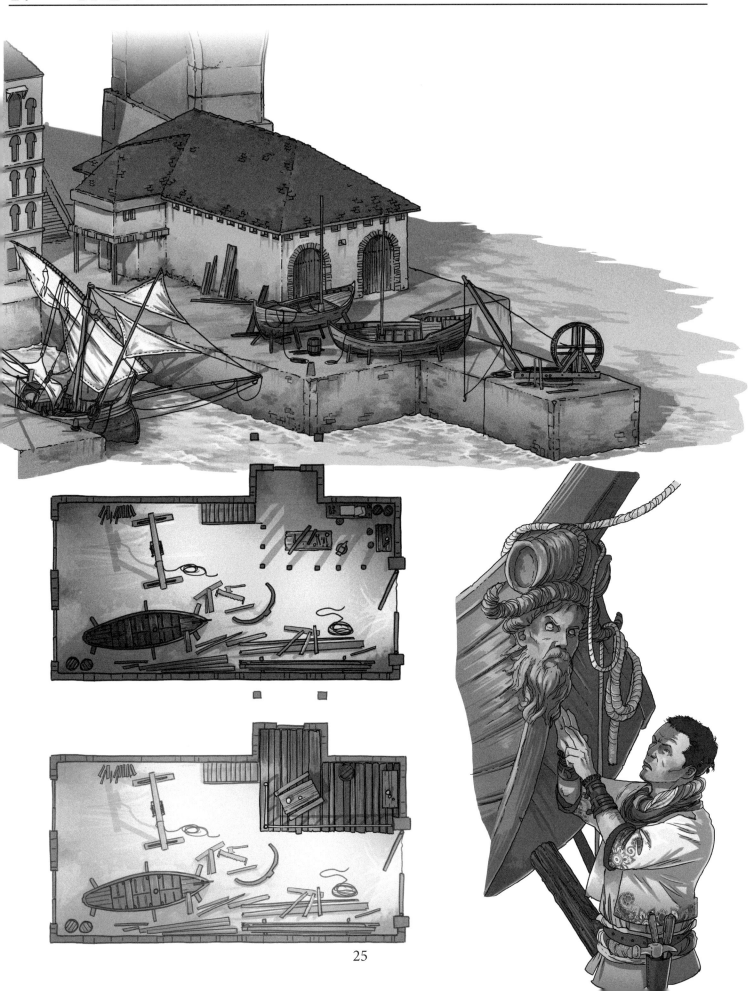

25

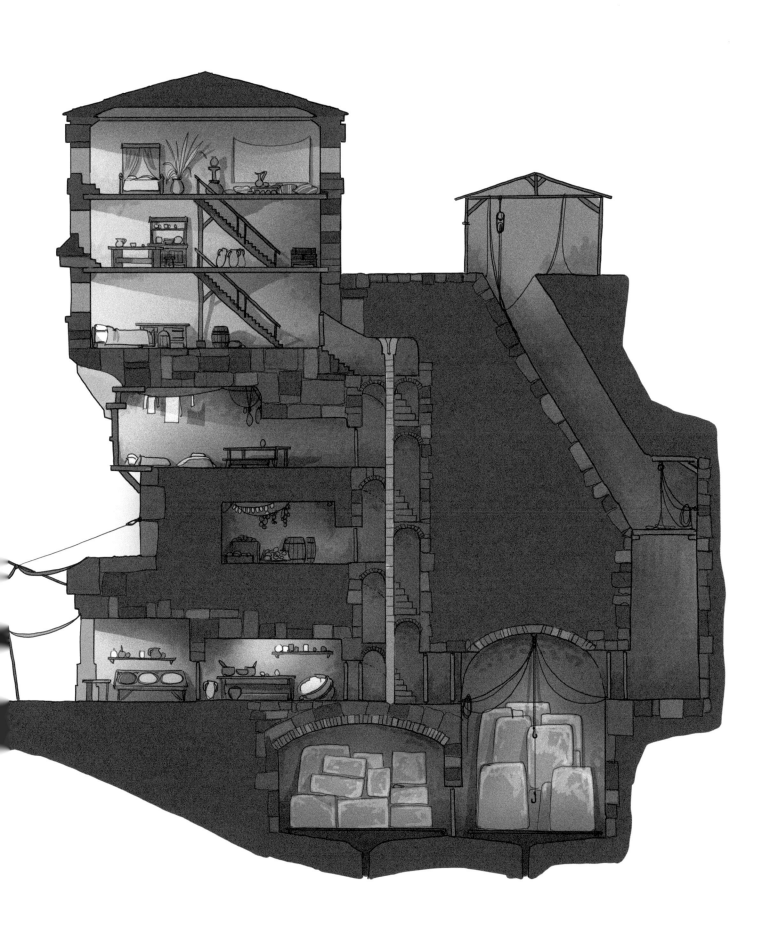

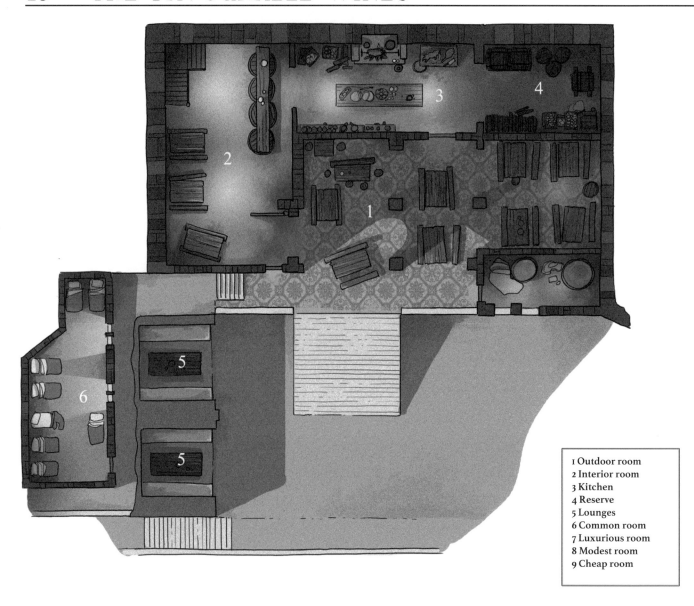

1 Outdoor room
2 Interior room
3 Kitchen
4 Reserve
5 Lounges
6 Common room
7 Luxurious room
8 Modest room
9 Cheap room

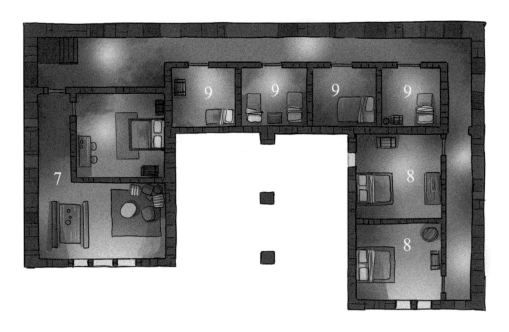

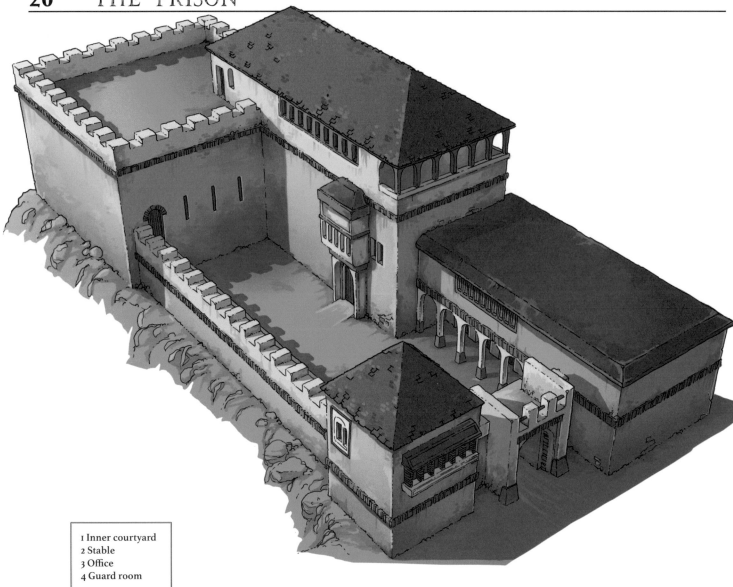

1 Inner courtyard
2 Stable
3 Office
4 Guard room

Ground floor

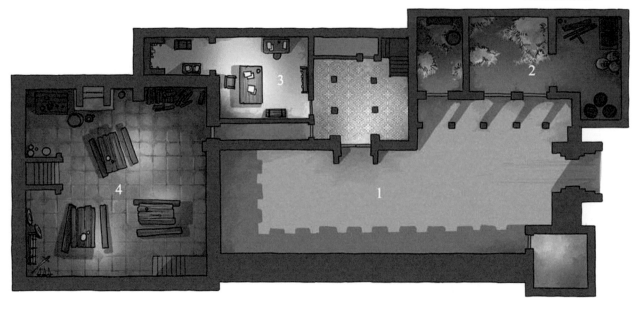

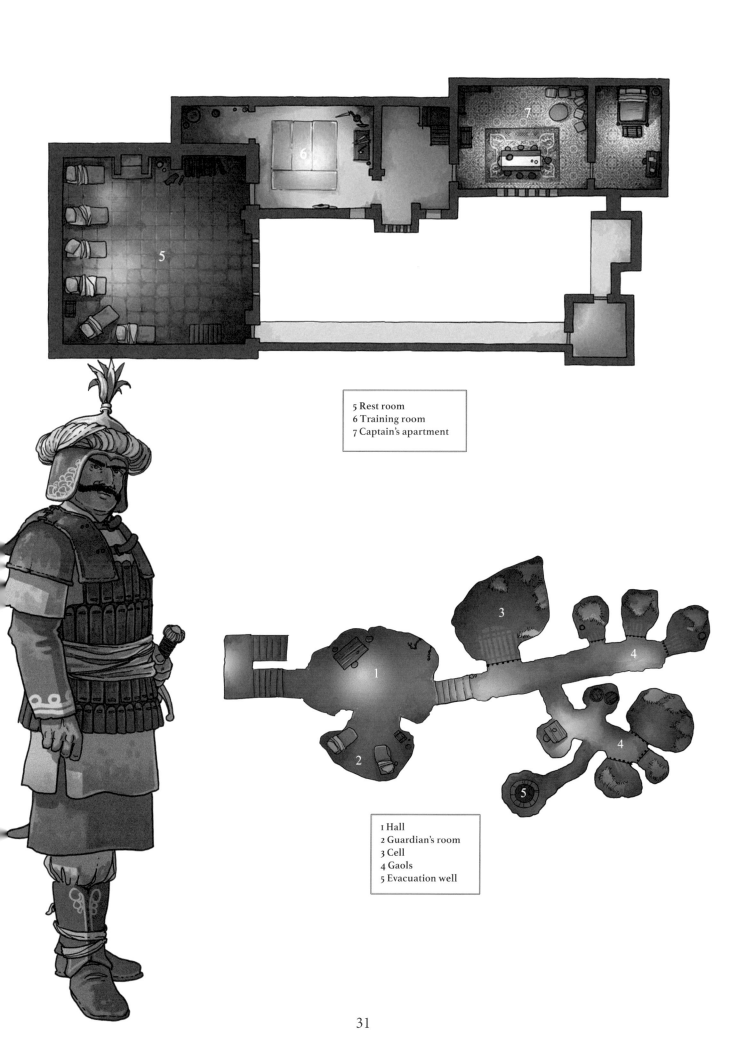

5 Rest room
6 Training room
7 Captain's apartment

1 Hall
2 Guardian's room
3 Cell
4 Gaols
5 Evacuation well

1 Stable
2 Salting room
3 Slaughterhouse
4 Apartment
5 Platform

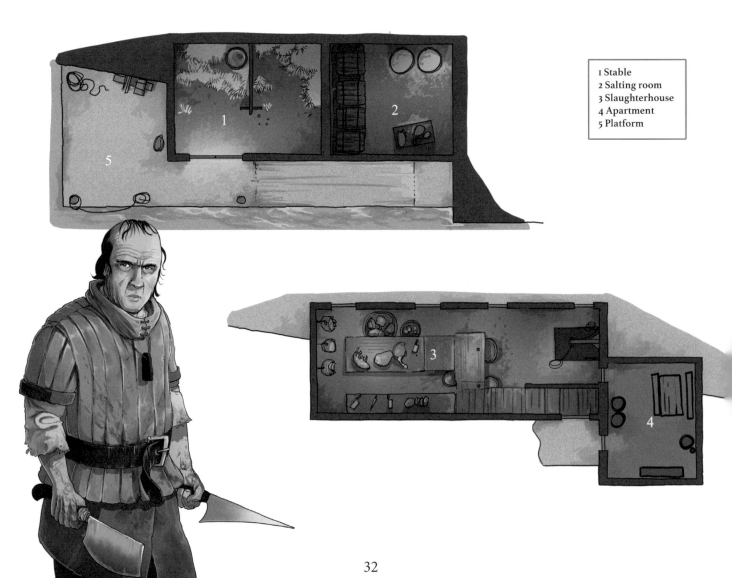

1 Room
2 Bedroom
3 Bedroom
4 Kitchen
5 Store

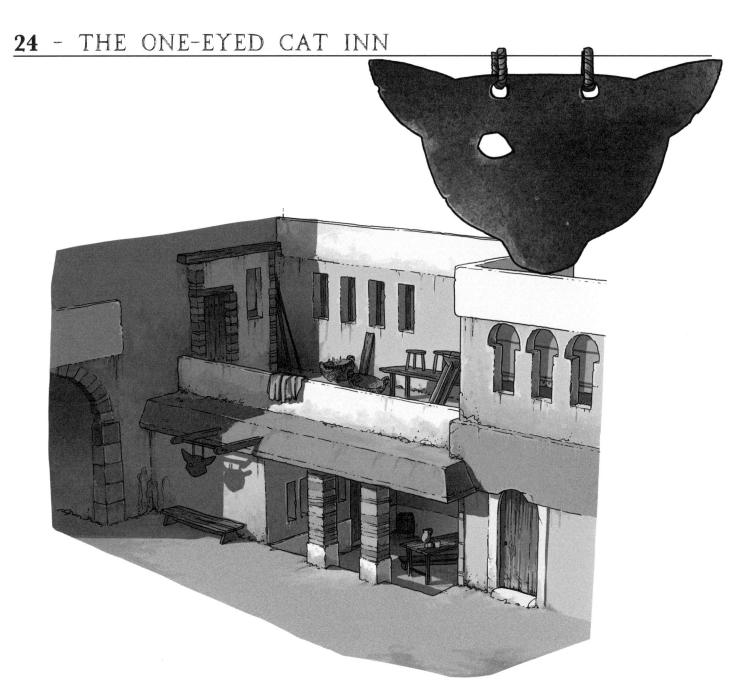

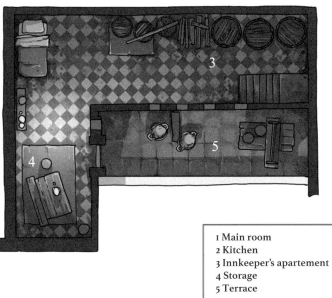

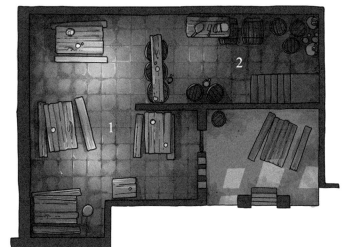

1 Main room
2 Kitchen
3 Innkeeper's apartement
4 Storage
5 Terrace

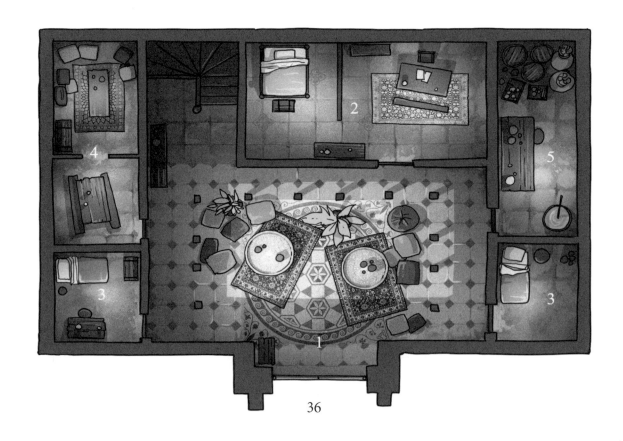

Ground floor

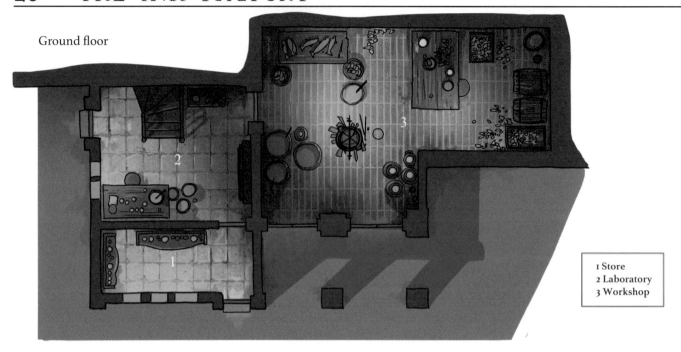

1 Store
2 Laboratory
3 Workshop

2nd floor

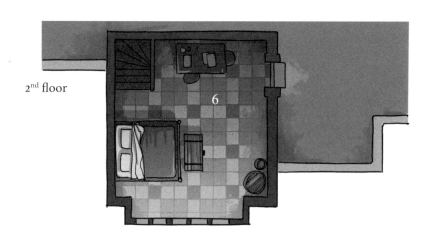

4 Room	
5 Bedroom	
6 Bedroom	

1st floor

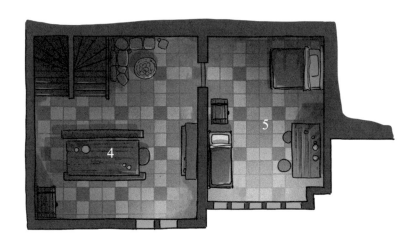

Street restaurant

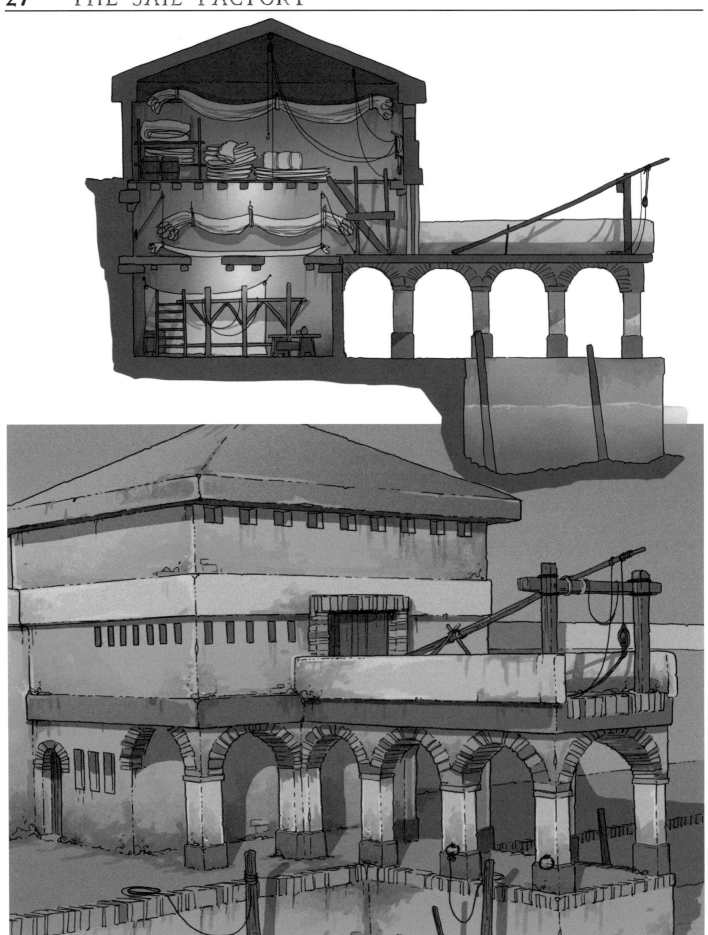

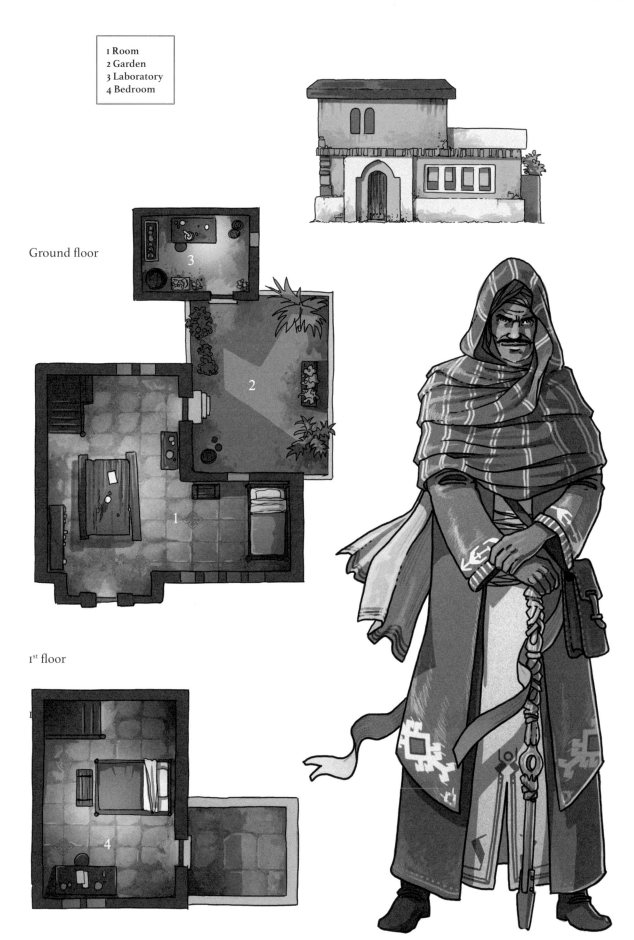

1 Room
2 Garden
3 Laboratory
4 Bedroom

Ground floor

1st floor

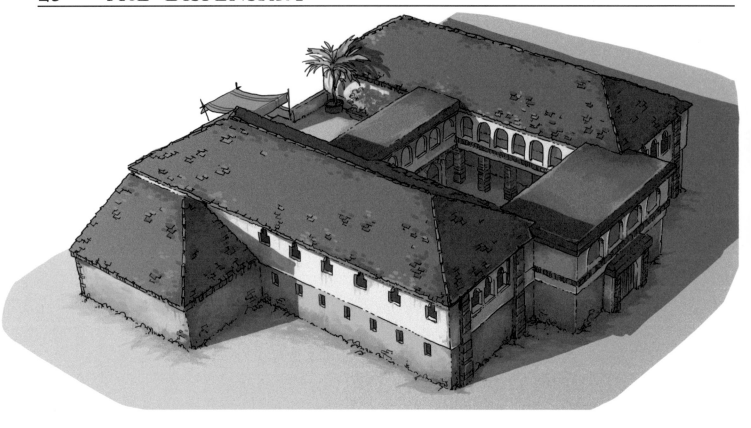

Ground floor

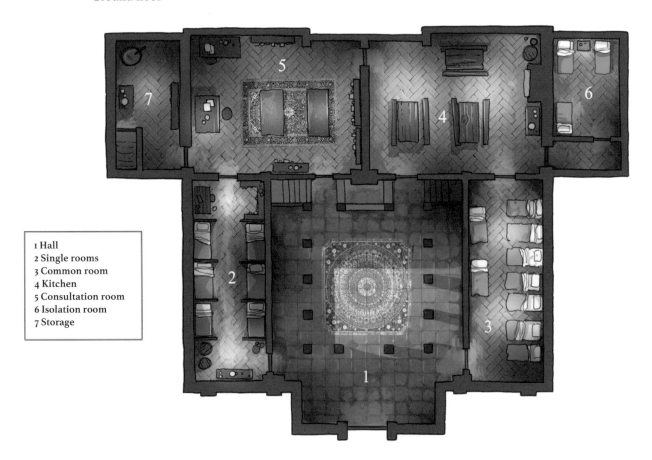

1 Hall
2 Single rooms
3 Common room
4 Kitchen
5 Consultation room
6 Isolation room
7 Storage

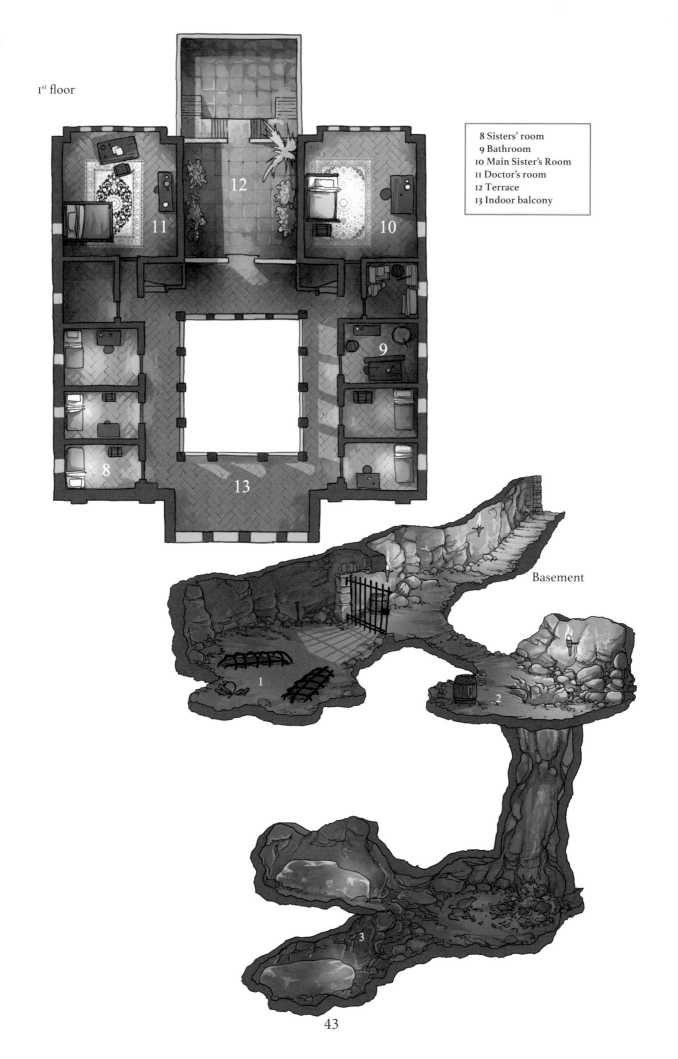

1st floor

8 Sisters' room
9 Bathroom
10 Main Sister's Room
11 Doctor's room
12 Terrace
13 Indoor balcony

11

12

10

9

8

13

Basement

1

2

3

1 The guardian's room
2 Room
3 Secret passage
4 Mine
5 Fountain